Magic Carpet

Magic carpet,
your bright colours
delight the eye.

Your moons and stars
and midnight blues
sing of the sky.

Magic carpet,
kept in the cupboard,
I hear you sigh.

Let me unroll
your magic pattern
and help you fly.

Tony Mitton

Young Hippo
Magic Poems

Compiled by Jennifer Curry

Illustrated by Philip Hopman

Hippo

This anthology is dedicated, with love, to my grandson
PETER CURRY
*in the hope that the whole of his life
will be touched by magic.*

Scholastic Children's Books,
Commonwealth House, 1-19 New Oxford Street,
London WC1A 1NU, UK
a division of Scholastic Ltd
London ~ New York ~ Toronto ~ Sydney ~ Auckland

Published in the UK by Scholastic Ltd, 1997

ISBN 0 590 19170 5

Printed by Cox & Wyman Ltd, Reading, Berks.

2 4 6 8 10 9 7 5 3 1

ᔕᕈ Contents ᔕᕈ

ᔕᕈ TASTER ᔕᕈ

Magic Carpet   *Tony Mitton*   1

ᔕᕈ FIRST WORD ᔕᕈ

Maybe Outside   *Cathy Vincent*   9

ᔕᕈ UNDER THE MAGIC TREE ᔕᕈ

Jack's Magic Wand   *David Harmer*   12

Where Can It Be?   *Mike Jubb*   14

Do You Want to Be a Wizard?   *Wes Magee*   15

Magpie Magic   *Patricia Leighton*   17

Tiny Elephants   *Tony Mitton*   19

The Path   *Jean Kenward*   21

What My Granny Did   *Jonathan Wakeham*   22

The King and Queen of China   *Jean Kenward*   24

The Three Singing Birds   *James Reeves*   26

The Marvellous Trousers   *Richard Edwards*   29

Magic the Rabbit   *David Harmer*   32

Merlin's Mynah   *Tony Mitton*   34

SPELL

Merlin's Spell to Make Broken Toys Happy   *Eric Johns*   36

❧ THE SWISH OF THE BROOMSTICKS ❧

Broomstick Obedience Class   *Daphne Schiller*   38

Witchy Kittens   *David Whitehead*   41

Charm Against an Egg-Boat   *Anon*   43

The Woolly Witch   *Celia Warren*   44

Hallowe'en   *Dawn Elizabeth Edwards*   45

Hallowe'en Disco   *David Whitehead*   47

Hallowe'en   *Dave Ward*   51

Riddle   *Marion Swinger*   54

The Which Hoo Cudn't Spel   *Mike Jubb*   55

SPELL

A Country Spell Against Witches   *Anon*   56

❧ GRICKLE GRACKLE GROOBLE GROBBLE ❧

Weed Soup   *Laura Ranger*   58

Double, Double   *William Shakespeare*   59

Cherry Croak   *Tony Mitton*   61

Going Shopping   *Paul Cookson*   63

Mummy?   *David Poulter*   65

Listen!   *Lilian Moore*   67

The Preston Witch   *Sara Jones*   68

The Witch's Work Song   *T.H. White*   69

Disappear   *Laura Ranger*   70

SPELL

Spell For Disappearing   *John Rice*   71

❧DRAGONS, GIANTS AND THE MAGIC SPIDERMAN❧

Dragonbirth   *Judith Nicholls*   73

The Sick Young Dragon   *John Foster*   75

Dragon Dance   *Max Fatchen*   78

Dragon Poem   *Frances Edwards*   80

Building a Dragon   *Charles Thomson*   81

Giant Taste   *Andrew Collett*   83

The Giant   *Anon*   83

The Sleepy Giant   *Charles Edward Carryl*   84

Giant   *Monica Campbell-Scott*   86

Anancy the Spiderman   *Manley Young*   87

SPELL

Merlin's Spell to Find Lost Toys   *Eric Johns*   89

❧SOMETHING QUEER❧

Eeka, Neeka   *Walter de la Mare*   91

Two Word Poem   *Laura Ranger*   92

I Wish   *Anon*   93

The Woman of Water   *Adrian Mitchell*   94

Lion   *Celia Warren*   96

Some Day, My Prince   *Mike Jubb*   99

Little Fan   *James Reeves*   100

Magic Cat   *Peter Dixon*   103

Lost Rainbow   *Peter Dixon*   105

SPELL

To Get Rid of Warts   *translated by Mike Rosen*   106

TREADING MY DREAMS

Dream Catcher   *Patricia Leighton*   109

You Spotted Snakes   *William Shakespeare*   110

Overheard on a Saltmarsh   *Harold Monro*   112

Who Believes in Fairies?   *Patricia Leighton*   114

On Midsummer's Eve   *Ann Bonner*   116

Coach   *Eleanor Farjeon*   118

Winter Window   *Gina Douthwaite*   120

Wizard   *Daphne Schiller*   121

Song of the Wizard's Imp   *Tony Mitton*   123

Dreams and Shadows   *Patricia Leighton*   125

LAST WORD

The Vanishing Poem   *Tim Pointon*   127

First Word

Maybe Outside

Go and open the door.
Maybe outside there's a dish
And on that dish is a silver fish
With waving fins in a golden light.

Go and open the door.
Maybe outside there's a princess
Wearing a beautiful dress
Singing a song about herself.

Go and open the door.
Maybe outside there's a magic toy box
With a dancing doll and talking sailors,
And an elephant which plays with you all the
     time.

Go and open the door.

Maybe outside there's a swimming-pool

With lots of laughing children in it.

Diving and swimming and playing.

Perhaps they'll let you join the fun.

Cathy Vincent (aged 8)

Under the Magic Tree

Jack's Magic Wand

"It really will work," said Jack yesterday
Just as our teacher was clearing away
"If I wave this wand and say the right words
That pile of Maths books will turn into birds."

Chalk powdered our hair, ink squirted our faces
The rulers and pencils began to run races.
Our teacher became a most elegant pig
Waving his trotters and dancing a jig.

"I got it for Christmas from my Uncle Stan
Such an amazing, mysterious man
He wears a long cloak, a tall pointed hat
A wizard of course, no doubt about that."

Our Headmaster was starting to shout
As giant erasers were rubbing him out
Miss Brown grew a beard, Miss Green turned red
With the caretaker's mop stuck on her head.

The school went so crazy it gave us a fright
But Jack's Uncle Stan made everything right
Except for one thing, a real disaster
He could not seem to return our Headmaster.

David Harmer

Where Can It Be?

A
long
time ago
there lived
a very old and
absent-minded
magician who was
always losing things,
especially his favourite hat.

Mike Jubb

Do You Want to Be a Wizard?

Do you want to be a wizard?
  Well, you'll need a pointed hat
  with silver stars and golden moon,
  and perched on top ... a bat.

Do you want to be a wizard?
  Well, you'll need *Ye Booke of Spells*
  and rotten eggs and fried frogs' legs
  to make some horrid smells.

Do you want to be a wizard?
  Well, you'll need some pickled brains,
  a wand, a cloak, and one dead rat,
  and green slime from the drains.

Do you *still* want to be a wizard?

Wes Magee

Magpie Magic

I saw a single magpie
and was sad it was not two.
I saw a pair of magpies
so my wish came true.
I saw three magpies
flying over me.
They dropped a letter at my feet.
What could it be?

I saw four magpies
with elf boys on their wings.
I saw five magpies
with five silver rings.
I saw six magpies
fly up to the sun
which sprinkled gold all over them.
They shone and shone.

I saw seven magpies
with a secret to tell
but what it was is mine and theirs –
to share would break the spell.

Patricia Leighton

Tiny Elephants

I've got elephants,
tiny little elephants,
hardly any bigger
than an ant
or a bee.

I've got elephants,
tiny little elephants.
And every single elephant
belongs to me.

I've got elephants,
tiny little elephants,
peeping from my pockets
and hiding in my hair.

I've got elephants,
but nobody can see them.
I'm the only person
who knows they're there.

Tony Mitton

The Path

There's a path through the woods
   that's magic.
It turns
    from left
  to right
in a shadowy mist
  of bluebells.
There's never a soul
  in sight,
but always
     the sound
of voices
whispering
  near and far,
and a scrabble of tiny
  footprints...
Whose do you guess
  they are?

Jean Kenward

What My Granny Did

This is what my granny did.
She used to just watch television,
And talk, and give me biscuits when I called.
But then she learned some magic
Not like magic I had ever seen.
She had no hankies blooming purple,
No wooden rabbits snuffling in a box,
But just herself, and magic.
She magicked herself thinner, smaller.
She magicked her house darker, sadder,
Till it no longer smelt of pear-drops
But of dust, and books, and empty kettles.
She magicked her voice to just a whisper,
Dry like biscuits,
And her smile to something far-off, stranger,
That only she could understand.

And then, one day,
She vanished, just like that,
And Dad cried at the brilliance of it all.

Jonathan Wakeham

The King and Queen of China

I had a fan;
I shook my fan,
it opened wide as wide.
The King and Queen of China
were sitting down
inside,

And she had a blue-green
peacock
(a bird with a blue-green tail),
and he had a golden head-dress
and a kite with a golden
sail.

I had a fan.
I shook my fan,
it folded tight and thin;
the King and Queen of China –
I shut them safely
in,

And soon, in a small
small whisper
I heard two voices say
"The King and Queen of China
went visiting
today!"

Jean Kenward

The Three Singing Birds

The King walked in his garden green,
    Where grew a marvellous tree;
And out of its leaves came singing birds
    By one, and two, and three.

The first bird had wings of white,
    The second had wings of gold,
The third had wings of deepest blue
    Most beauteous to behold.

The white bird flew to the northern land,
    The gold bird flew to the west,
The blue bird flew to the cold, cold south
    Where never bird might nest.

The King waited a twelvemonth long,
    Till back the three birds flew,
They lighted down upon the tree,
    The white, the gold, and the blue.

The white bird brought a pearly seed
  And gave it to the King;
The gold bird from out of the west
  He brought a golden ring.

The third bird with feathers blue
  Who came from the far cold south,
A twisted sea-shell smooth and grey
  He carried in his mouth.

The King planted the pearly seed
  Down in his garden green,
And up there sprang a pearl-white maid,
  The fairest ever seen.

She looked at the King and knelt her down
  All under the magic tree,
She smiled at him with her red lips
  But not a word said she.

Instead she took the grey sea-shell
    And held it to his ear,
She pressed it close and soon the King
    A strange, sweet song did hear.

He raised the fair maid by the hand
    Until she stood at his side;
Then he gave her the golden ring
    And took her for his bride.

And at their window sang the birds,
    They sang the whole night through,
Then off they went at break of day,
    The white, the gold, and the blue.

James Reeves

The Marvellous Trousers

Last week on my way to a friend's birthday tea
I found them draped over the branch of a tree,
Oh, the Marvellous Trousers.

One leg was striped silver, the other striped
   blue;
I put them on, closed my eyes, wished and
   then flew!
Oh, the Marvellous Trousers.

They carried me up like a rocket, so fast
I ruffled the tail of each pigeon I passed,
Oh, the Marvellous Trousers.

I soared over Sicily, rolled over Rome,

And circled the Eiffel Tower on my way home,

Oh, the Marvellous Trousers.

I landed with ribbons of cloud in my hair,

But when I looked down at my legs – they
were bare!

Oh, no Marvellous Trousers.

I know it sounds funny, I know it sounds
weird,

But somehow and somewhere they'd just
disappeared,

Oh, the Marvellous Trousers.

And when I explained at my friend's birthday
  tea,
The guests shook their heads and blew
  raspberries at me,
Oh, the Marvellous Trousers.

But I don't care tuppence: I've rolled over Rome,
I've circled the Eiffel Tower on my way home,
I've worn the Marvellous Trousers,
The Marvellous, Marvellous Trousers!

Richard Edwards

Magic the Rabbit

My rabbit is called Magic
Not just because he wrinkles his nose
And carrots disappear.

Not just because
He wriggles right under the straw
At the back of his hutch
And he disappears.

Not just because
Every time my football team wins
He leaps up and down.

But because last week
He turned the milkman into a frog
The paper girl into a walrus
The postman into a purple jelly
The dustman into a giant lemon
And made my mum and dad
King and Queen of all the World
and me Prime Minister.

"That's magic, Magic," we cheered
Once we'd wished them all back again
"Really magic."

David Harmer

Merlin's Mynah

I'm Misty the Mynah, haven't you heard?
I'm Merlin's marvellous talking bird.

I sit in his study where I'm warm and fed,
and I hear every single word that's said.

I store it all in my small bird-brain
till I want to call it back again.

I can conjure up whatever I need:
a nice new perch or the best bird seed.

Or if I feel like a bit of fun
I can speak a spell to get things done.

I can magic a spider in Merlin's tea,
I can make his cornflakes cry, "Hee, hee, hee!"

When he's reading a book I can lose his page,
I can tickle his ear till he gets in a rage.

I can fly his hat right up in the air,
I can make him tumble when he sits in a chair.

And why should he put up with all of my tricks?
Well, without old Misty, *he'd* be in a fix.

Poor old Merlin, haven't you heard?
He can never remember a single word.

It may sound crazy, it may seem absurd,
but I'm Misty the Mynah, his memory bird!

Tony Mitton

Spell

Merlin's Spell to Make Broken Toys Happy

hairless

armless

legless

eyeless

– I will make you smile again

furless

earless

wheel-less

squeakless

– I will love you all the same

Say this spell very quietly and stroke the broken toy gently with your wand. This spell always works.

Eric Johns

The Swish of the Broomsticks

Broomstick Obedience Class

I ordered my broom to lift and fly,
It whizzed like a firework into the sky

But left me behind in an angry heap
Pretending to laugh in order to keep

My cool in front of the other witches
Who were creasing themselves into terrible
   stitches.

"Come back at once!" I shouted out,
But then it behaved like a playground lout

Bashing the other brooms on purpose,
Turning the class to a riotous circus

With witches tumbling through the air,
Their black hats spinning everywhere.
The cats were dropping in free fall,
Spitting in fury at one and all.

The teacher tried to keep things calm
And summoned my broom, but to my alarm

It walloped him over the head and chest
Then brushed him into a pile with the rest.

The broom was expelled from the class that day,
But later on I got my way.

I turned it into a vacuum cleaner
Which made my image a whole lot meaner.

Now I buzz across the night-time sky
Sucking up clouds as I pass by.

Daphne Schiller

Witchy Kittens

The witch's cat had kittens
One dark and spooky night.
A night as black as beetles' backs
With never a chink of light.

She washed them and she fed them
And kept them close and warm
She stayed awake the long, long night
To see they took no harm.

She coddled them and cuddled them
And licked them clean and dry
She gave them little sips of milk
To still their mewing cry.

Although she could not see a thing
'Twas as black as witches' hats
She counted seven tiny tails
On seven tiny cats.

"I must name my seven babies –
Names all dark and witchy –
I'll call them Ebony, Midnight, Inky, Jet,
Licquorice, Charcoal and Pitchy."

Then when she'd named her family
She purred and slept till light
At crack of dawn she woke to find
HER SEVEN BLACK BABES WERE WHITE

David Whitehead

Charm Against an Egg-Boat

You must break the shell to bits, for fear
The witches should make it a boat, my dear:
For over the sea, away from home,
Far by night the witches roam.

Anon

(There is an old belief that when you eat a boiled egg
you should put a hole in the unbroken end of the shell.
If you don't, then a witch might steal it, turn it into a
boat and row out to sea to start a storm!)

The Woolly Witch

I'm the wicked woolly witch,
When knitting needles start to twitch
I cast a wicked woolly spell:
"Knit one, purl one,   a stitch!"
                    d
                      r
                    o
                  p

Celia Warren

Hallowe'en

The witches fly in the moonlight,
with long dark purple cloaks
Streaming behind them.
The cackles and screams,
their black cats spitting
their chins almost touching their broomsticks,
I saw them on Hallowe'en.
Beyond the weird ghostly enchanted forest.
The wizards flying by the power
of their long black cloaks.
The trees with boughs bending
over you as if you
were prisoners of the wood.
The rushing rivers rushing
with the North Wind.
The fog spreading,
I saw all this on Hallowe'en.

The witches collecting
fog and mist and midnight air.
Moonlight too.
The goblins, ghouls, sprites
trolls and pixies creeping
out of mossy damp green holes.
I saw all this from my bedroom window.
The spiders amongst
the twigs and branches of the trees
spinning webs.
Skeletons (Men) and ghosts (Ladies)
walking together arm in arm.
I saw all this from my bedroom window.

Dawn Elizabeth Edwards (aged 7)

Hallowe'en Disco

The witches are gathering
stay safely indoors
as the swish of the broomsticks
is heard from the tors
as the evil ones all swoop down from the moors.

There's Mag from the mountain
and Meg from the mill
humpty-back Hannah
and single-eyed Jill
crawled up from their caverns under the hill.

Don't go out – don't go out – don't take the
   risk Oh!
the witches are having their Hallowe'en disco.

They're down in the wild-wood
deep in the trees
dancing and prancing
341 elbows and knees
as nightmarish music floats up on the breeze.

There's a trio of zombies
howling a tune
as a grisly ghost
is starting to croon
in the bright chilly light of the Hallowe'en moon.

Lock your door – lock your door – don't take
  the risk Oh!
the witches and warlocks are having a disco.

Skeleton waiters
are serving the food
like man-off-the-bone
and cockroaches stewed
with bat's-blood cola – specially brewed.

Real toad-in-the-hole
is the dish of the day
there's barbecued lizard
and snake baked in clay

You'll be on the menu if you don't keep away.

Stay at home – stay at home – don't take the
     risk Oh!
the witches are having their Hallowe'en disco.

But when the dawn starts to break
they'll be gone never fear
back to their witcheries
some far and some near
But remember, remember –

They'll be back here next year.

David Whitehead

Hallowe'en

it's a black plastic bin bag
that flaps around my shoulders
it's a cardboard mask
that covers my face
and I don't believe in witches
or werewolves or zombies
I'm just out here making mischief
with my mates

shrieking round the keyholes
chanting "trick or treat" –
a quick way to raise some coppers
or some sweets –
or if they're tight and chase us
they know we'll just come back
and chuck pebbles up the windows
or soapy water in their face

but I don't know why we do it
it's just a laugh
and I don't believe in witches
like I said
but then I wonder what my mates see
every time they look at me –
do I look as strange as they do
in the dark?

and out there
beyond the streetlamps
and the houselights
and the tellies
where the dark fields slide down
towards the river
can't you feel something waking
something watching
something waiting
something crawling up the alleys
while we clutch each other's hands
and watch the flickering candles
in the withered pumpkin heads
go out like dying stars
as we stand and shiver?

Dave Ward

Riddle

Can you make a witch itch?

Take away her W
then she'll cease to trouble you.

Marion Swinger

The Which Hoo Cudn't Spel

There wunce woz a which hoo cudn't spel,
She sed she didn't mind;
She maid mor mistakes than I cud tel,
How meny can **you** find?

Mike Jubb

Spell

A Country Spell Against Witches

Blackthorn bark and poppy seed,

Thistledown and water-weed,

Send the witches off with speed.

Anon

GRICKLE

GRACKLE

GROOBLE

GROBBLE

MUNCH
MUNCH
MUNCH

Weed Soup

For magic powers,
mix together
four cherry blossom leaves
and nine pink flowers.
Wait for three hours.

Walk slowly in the flower beds.
Find seven white daisies
and two dried lavender heads.
Throw in one dandelion,
ten geranium petals,
and eight sprigs of mint.
Take five ferns plus
one handful of baby tears.
Add sand and water.
Stir for years and years.

Warning:
Children do not eat this soup

Laura Ranger (aged 7)

Double, Double, Toil and Trouble

Double, double, toil and trouble;
Fire burn and cauldron bubble.

Round about the cauldron go;
In the poisoned entrails throw.
Toad, that under cold stone
Days and nights has thirty-one
Swelter'd venom sleeping got,
Boil thou first i' the charmed pot.

Double, double, toil and trouble;
Fire burn and cauldron bubble.

Fillet of a fenny snake,
In the cauldron boil and bake;
Eye of newt and toe of frog,
Wool of bat and tongue of dog,
Adder's fork and blindworm's sting,
Lizard's leg and howlet's wing,
For a charm of powerful trouble
Like a hell-broth boil and bubble.

Double, double, toil and trouble;
Fire burn and cauldron bubble.

William Shakespeare
from *Macbeth*

Cherry Croak (or Raiding the Wizard's Kitchen)

Cor!

I wonder what this is for?

It's all red and fizzy,

just like Cherry Coke

(except for the smoke...)

Hmmmm...

cool as ice.

Mmmmm...

smells nice.

Think, maybe

I'll try a sip.

Oooh! Bubbles bursting

on my lip –

Pop! Pop! Pop!

Heeeeey! Everything's taller.
Oh, no. It's me that's getting smaller.
Oooh! *Hop! Hop! Hop!*
Well, I'm blowed!
I've turned into a toad.
That was no Coke.
And this is no joke.
Croak, croak, croak...

Tony Mitton

Going Shopping With Willy the Wise and Wizened Wizard

Every Saturday Willy the wise and wizened
  wizard
went into town to do his weekly shopping.

He'd get his toiletries from Roots the Alchemist,
his clothes from Sparks and Mensa,
new ideas for games and tricks from Ploys R Us
and his food from the supermarket – usually
  Asda,
because he thought it sounded like a magic
  word...
"Asda Cadabra!"

His special ingredients and potion mixtures,
the secret things on his list like

17 newts' eyes, 21 frog tongues,
36 bat wings, 15 hog warts,
3 witch pimples, 9 rattlesnake rattles,
one kg of six-inch pins,
3 bags of all-purpose filler and mixer
plus a new universal scoop, stirrer
and spreader

Well, Willy the wise and wizened wizard
got them from a specialist shop:
Voodoo It All – The Druid Yourself Store.

Paul Cookson

Mummy?

"Mummy?
  Do ogres
    live in our garden shed?"

"Of course not dear."

"Mummy?
  Do ogres
    have enormous fangs?"

"Of course not dear."

"Mummy?
  Do ogres
    dribble when they eat?"

"Of course not dear."

"Mummy?
  Do ogres
    crunch and crack your bones?"

"Of course not dear."

"Mummy?
  Well...
    What's that
      gobbling up our dad?"

David Poulter

Listen!

Listen to the witch!

grinch grinch
grunch
chip-chop
crunch

grickle
grackle
grooble
grobble

munch
munch
munch

Whatever in the world
is she having for lunch?

Lilian Moore

The Preston Witch

There was an old witch from Preston,
Who asked herself this question,
Was it the rats,
The snails or the bats,
That gave her acute indigestion?

Sara Jones (aged 9)

The Sick Young Dragon

"What can I do?" Young Dragon cried.
"Although I've simply tried and tried
It doesn't matter how hard I blow,
I cannot get my fire to go!"

"Open your mouth!" his mother said,
"It's no wonder! Your throat's not red.
Your scales are cold. You must be ill.
I think you might have caught a chill."

The doctor came. He looked and said,
"You'll need a day or two in bed.
Your temperature's down. No doubt
That's the reason your fire's gone out.

"Just drink this petrol. Chew these nails.
They'll help you to warm up your scales.
Just take it easy. Watch TV,
You'll soon be right as rain, you'll see."

Young Dragon did as he was told
And soon his scales stopped feeling cold.
He sneezed some sparks. His face glowed
  bright.
He coughed and set the sheets alight.

"Oh, dear!" he cried. "I've burnt the bed!"
"It doesn't matter," his mother said.
"Those sheets were old. Go out and play.
Just watch where you breathe fire today."

John Foster

Dragon Dance

A Chinese dragon's in the street
And dancing on its Chinese feet
With fearsome head and golden scale
And twisting its ferocious tail.
Its bulging eyes are blazing red
While smoke is puffing from its head
And well you nervously might ask
What lies behind that fearful mask.

It twists and twirls across the road
While BANG the cracker strings explode.
Don't yell or run or shout or squeal
Or make a Chinese dragon's meal
For, where its heated breath is fired
They say it likes to be admired.
With slippered joy and prancing shoe
Why, you can join the dragon too.
There's fun with beating gongs and din
When dragons dance the New Year in.

Max Fatchen

Dragon Poem

He comes in the night, killing all greenery,
with his spiky tail and rough scabby skin
killing all the humans and spitting the bones
  in the bin.

Frances Edwards (aged 11)

Building a Dragon

Once I built a dragon
Three times the size of you.
I made him out of cardboard
and chicken wire and glue.

It took me weeks and weeks and weeks
until I got him right.
I hid him in the loft by day
and worked on him at night.

The cardboard came from boxes
I asked the grocer for.
I borrowed tins of paint
from Mr Brown next door.

It took me weeks and weeks and weeks
(well, four at least – no, five!)
and then I got a nasty shock:
the dragon came alive.

It burst out through the roof –
so I could see the stars –
went crashing down the road
and damaged several cars.

I've looked for him for weeks and weeks.
Where did my dragon go?
If anyone has seen him, will
they kindly let me know?

Charles Thomson

82

Giant Taste

A giant crunched a car
two lorries and a tram,
to sample all the flavours
of delicious traffic jam.`

Andrew Collett

The Giant

Fee, fie, fo, fum!
I smell the blood of an English man.
Be he alive, or be he dead,
I'll grind his bones to make my bread.

Anon

The Sleepy Giant

My age is three hundred and seventy-two,
   And I think, with the deepest regret,
How I used to pick up and voraciously chew
   The dear little boys whom I met.

I've eaten them raw, in their holiday suits;
   I've eaten them curried with rice;
I've eaten them baked, in their jackets and
   boots,
   And found them exceedingly nice.

But now that my jaws are too weak for such
fare,
   I think it exceedingly rude
To do such a thing, when I'm quite well aware
   Little boys do not like to be chewed.

And so I contentedly live upon eels,
   And try to do nothing amiss,
And I pass all the time I can spare from my
meals
   In innocent slumber – like this.

Charles Edward Carryl

Giant

Big as a dinosaur,
Gentle as a flower,
Hopping like the sea crashing down,
A giant running through the sand,
Scrunching the stones,
Crying, making a swimming-pool with his tears.

Monica Campbell-Scott (aged 6)

Anancy the Spiderman

Anancy is a spider, Anancy is a man,
Anancy is West Indian an West African.
Anancy sailed to Englan on a banana boat,
An when he got to Brixton, everybody gave a
  shout.

Anancy! Anancy!
Anancy the magic spiderman.
Anancy! Anancy!
Anancy an Brer Englishman.
Anancy! Anancy!
Anancy the magic spiderman.
Anancy! Anancy!
Anancy an Brer Englishman.

Anancy is a jiver, he's frisky as a fly.
A shifty, plastic being, an that is no lie.
Anancy is a trickster, he's sensitive to guile,
He sometimes can be like a very greedy chile.

Anancy! Anancy...!

Manley Young

Spell

Merlin's Spell to Find Lost Toys

Mustily dustily
    under the stairs
squashily squeezily
    down the settee
higgily piggily
    in the toy box
blackily scratchily
    down the floorboards
ruffily ruggily
    under my bed

I can see you in my head

Remember to keep your eyes closed while you cast
this spell and think very hard about the last time
you saw the lost toy. Tap yourself on the head
with your wand – gently, of course. **Merlin**

Eric Johns

Something Queer

Eeka, Neeka

Eeka, Neeka, Leeka, Lee –
Here's a lock without a key;
Bring a lantern, bring a candle,
Here's a door without a handle;
Shine, shine, you old thief Moon,
Here's a door without a room;
Not a whisper, moth or mouse,
Key – lock – door – room: where's the house?

Say nothing, creep away,
And live to knock another day!

Walter de la Mare

Two Word Poem

The toad sat on a red stool
it was a toadstool.

The rain tied a bow
in the cloud's hair
it was a rainbow.

Which witch put sand
in my sandwich?

I stood under the bridge,
then I understood.

I sat on the ledge and
thought about what I know.
It was knowledge.

Laura Ranger (aged 7)

I Wish

I wish that my room had a floor
I don't care so much for a door;
But this walking around
Without touching the ground
Is getting to be quite a bore.

Anon

The Woman of Water

There once was a woman of water
Refused a Wizard her hand.
So he took the tears of a statue
And the weight from a grain of sand
And he squeezed the sap from a comet
And the height from a cypress tree
And he drained the dark from midnight
And he charmed the brains from a bee
And he soured the mixture with thunder
And he stirred it with ice from hell
And the woman of water drank it down
And she changed into a well.

There once was a woman of water
Who was changed into a well
And the well smiled up at the Wizard
And down down that old Wizard fell...

Adrian Mitchell

Lion

I have a box
in which I keep
a shoulder I may cry on,
I lift the lid
and there inside's
a large and lovely lion.

My lion is wild
with glorious mane,
a pounce in every paw,
I have to keep
him in a box
for fear that he may roar.

The box is small,
you'd hardly think
the King of Beasts would fit,
I only keep
my lion there
by training him to sit.

From time to time
I lift the lid
to hear my lion purr,
and gently stroke
my fingers through
his soft and friendly fur.

I have a box
in which I keep
a secret to rely on,
so carefully close
the lid upon
my large and lovely lion.

Celia Warren

Some Day, My Prince...

Kiss ..... Croak

Kiss ..... Croak

Kiss ..... Croak

Kiss ..... Croak

I'll find that flipping Prince
if I have to kiss
every frog in this pond.

Mike Jubb

Little Fan

"I don't like the look of little Fan, mother,
  I don't like her looks a little bit.
Her face – well, it's not exactly different,
  But there's something wrong with it.

"She went down to the sea-shore yesterday,
  And she talked to somebody there,
Now she won't do anything but sit
  And comb out her yellowy hair.

"Her eyes are shiny and she sings, mother,
  Like nobody ever sang before.
Perhaps they gave her something queer to eat,
  Down by the rocks on the shore.

"Speak to me, speak, little Fan dear,
  Aren't you feeling very well?
Where have you been and what are you singing,
  And what's that seaweedy smell?

"Where did you get that shiny comb, love,
  And those pretty coral beads so red?
Yesterday you had two legs, I'm certain,
  But now there's something else instead.

"I don't like the looks of little Fan, mother,
  You'd best go and close the door.
Watch now, or she'll be gone for ever
  To the rocks by the brown sandy shore."

James Reeves

Magic Cat

My mum whilst walking through the door
spilt some magic on the floor
blobs of this
and splats of that –
but most of it upon the cat.
Our cat turned magic – straight away –
and in the garden ran to play
where it grew two whopping wings
  and flew around in great big rings.

"Oh look!" cried Mother, "in the sky.
I didn't know the cat could fly..."

Then with a dash of Tibby's tail
it turned my mum into a snail!
So now she lives beneath a stone
and dusts around a different home –
   and I'm an ant
   and Dad's a mouse
and Tibby's living in our house.

Peter Dixon

Lost Rainbow

One day
coming home from school
(where else?)
I found a rainbow.

Lost
and sad
and torn
and broken
on a garage forecourt.
I picked it up,
wrapped it in a Wonderloaf wrapper
(which was also lost)
and took it home
where I warmed it
and dried it
in front of my mother's fire.
But it died.
I think it must have been
a very old rainbow.

Peter Dixon

Spell

A Very Old Spell to Say Out Loud to Get Rid of Warts

Wart, wart, wart–chicken

you must not start building here

you must not have a house here

you must head north from here

to the nearest hill

where, horrible thing

you have a brother.

He will put a leaf by your head.

Oh wither forever

under the foot of a wolf

under the eagle's wing

under the eagle's claw.

Die like coal in the fireplace

shrink like dung on the wall

dry up like water in a jug.

Become as small as a grain of linseed

smaller even than a skin-worm's hip-bone.

Become so small

that

you

become

nothing.

Anon
(translated from Middle English by
Michael Rosen)

Treading My Dreams

Dream Catcher

Over my bed is a delicate net
woven of silky silver thread.
Its tiny glass beads
bright raindrops are
and the gem in its centre
glows like a star.

A magical spider's web,
it is there
to trap evil dreams
and keep me from care.
But the good dreams
it sprinkles down on my head
so I dream in peace
in my soft, warm bed.

Patricia Leighton

According to legend, dream catchers were
given to Native Americans by the spirit of Spider.

You Spotted Snakes

You spotted snakes with double tongue,
  Thorny hedgehogs, be not seen;
Newts and blind-worms, do no wrong;
  Come not near our fairy queen.
    Philomel, with melody,
    Sing in our sweet lullaby;
Lulla, lulla, lullaby; lulla, lulla, lullaby!
    Never harm,
    Nor spell nor charm,
Come our lovely lady nigh;
So, good night, with lullaby.

Weaving spiders, come not here;
  Hence, you long legg'd spinners, hence!
Beetles black, approach not near;
  Worm nor snail, do no offence.

    Philomel, with melody,
    Sing in our sweet lullaby;
  Lulla, lulla, lullaby; lulla, lulla, lullaby!
    Never harm,
    Nor spell nor charm,
  Come our lovely lady nigh;
  So, good night, with lullaby!

William Shakespeare
from *A Midsummer Night's Dream*

Overheard on a Saltmarsh

Nymph, nymph, what are your beads?

Green glass, goblin. Why do you stare at them?

Give them me.

No.

Give them me. Give them me.

No.

Then I will howl all night in the reeds.
Lie in the mud and howl for them.

Goblin, why do you love them so?

They are better than stars or water,
Better than voices of winds that sing,
Better than any man's fair daughter,
Your green glass beads on a silver ring.

Hush, I stole them out of the moon.

Give me your beads. I desire them.

No.

I will howl in a deep lagoon
For your green glass beads, I love them so.
Give them me. Give them.

No.

Harold Monro

Who Believes in Fairies?

No one believes in fairies now,
tiny flittery things
with see-through wings.
No one believes they are true.
I don't. Do you?

Well – sometimes –
on summer nights
when the patio door is open
and the breeze makes strange
noises among the trees;
when the stars glitter
and silver moonshine
sparkles and flashes
between the leaves;
when our dog on the lawn
sits dead still
and stares, just stares
at thin air – well –
I do wonder.

Patricia Leighton

On Midsummer's Eve

The night
is hot
and still not
dark

moths make
circles
intent on
the light.

Tonight
we're told
the shy fairies
show themselves

the elves
will dance
round the magic
ring.

What a wonderful
thing!
Whether you
believe
in them
or not.

Ann Bonner

Coach

There was a yellow pumpkin
Born on a pumpkin patch,
As clumsy as a 'potamus,
As coarse as cottage-thatch.
It longed to be a gooseberry,
A greengage, or a grape,
It longed to give another scent
And have another shape.
The roses looked askance at it,
The lilies looked away –
"This thing is neither fruit nor flower!"
Their glances seemed to say.

One shiny night of midsummer,
When even fairies poach,
A good one waved her wand and said,
"O Pumpkin! be a coach!"
A coach of gold! a coach of glass!
A coach with satin lined!
If you should seek a thousand years,
Such you would not find.
The Princess in her crystal shoes
Eager for the dance
Stepped inside the pumpkin-coach
And rolled to her romance.

The roses reached out after it,
The lilies looked its way –
"O that we were pumpkins too!"
Their glances seemed to say.

Eleanor Farjeon

Winter Window

Frosted fairies, powder-light,
feathered their tiny wings, last night,
across my winter window,

carved a crystal paradise
of snowflake patterns and bracken in ice,
across my winter window,

blew cold, rolling scrolls and curls
that froze to etch an Arctic world
across my winter window.

Gina Douthwaite

Wizard

I am a wizard.
I live in a twisting tower.

My beard is eating my face
And my glasses won't settle.

My robe is on fire with planets,
My hat is busy with stars.

My staff speaks magic.
It crackles and sings.

I have no companion
Except for my owl.

Daphne Schiller

Song of the Wizard's Imp

Catch me if you can,
I'm a whisper of air,
a splinter of sunlight
that's gone if you stare.

Catch me if you can,
I'm a shadowy patch,
a rustle of cobweb
that's gone if you snatch.

Catch me if you can,
but be sure that you dare,
for I nestle to rest
in a wizard's warm hair.

Yes, catch me if you can,
but be warned I am weird,
for I settle to sleep
in the wizard's white beard.

Oh, catch me if you can,
but don't wake the wizard.
He'll glare and he'll growl
and you'll end up a lizard.

Tony Mitton

Dreams and Shadows

Unicorn
with one single
golden horn.

Unicorn
white in the moonlight
haunting the orchard
like a gentle ghost.

Unicorn
shadowy horse
cantering in and out
beneath scented branches.

Unicorn
treading my dreams
your eyes wide
your breath soft in my ears.

Unicorn
come – let me touch
your magic horn.

Keep quite still
while I wish.

Patricia Leighton

Last Word

The Vanishing Poem

A young poem once fell
under a terrible spell
which made it shrink

and shrink

until there

was so

little

ink

that

it

...

Tim Pointon

Acknowledgements

The compiler and publishers would like to thank the following for permission to use copyright material in this collection. The publishers have made every effort to contact the copyright holders but there are a few cases where it has not been possible to do so. We would be grateful to hear from anyone who can enable us to contact them so that the omission can be corrected at the first opportunity.

Ann Bonner for "On Midsummer's Eve" from *Let's Celebrate*, pub. OUP ~ Monica Campbell-Scott for "Giant" from *Wondercrump Poetry*, pub. Random House Children's Books ~ Andrew Collett for "Giant Taste" ~ Paul Cookson for "Going Shopping" ~ Peter Dixon for "Lost Rainbow" and "Magic Cat" from *Grow Your Own Rainbow*, pub. Thomas Nelson ~ Gina Douthwaite for "Winter Window" ~ Gerald Duckworth & Co Ltd for "Overheard on a Saltmarsh" by Harold Monro ~ Max Fatchen for "Dragon Dance" from *Let's Celebrate*, pub. OUP ~ John Foster for "The Sick Young Dragon" from *A Very First Poetry Book,* pub. OUP ~ David Harmer for "Jack's Magic Set" and "Magic the Rabbit" ~ David Higham Associates for "The Witch's Work Song" by T.H. White from *Sword in the Stone,* pub. HarperCollins; and for "Coach" by Eleanor Farjeon, from *Then There Were Three,* pub. Michael Joseph ~ Eric Johns for "Merlin's Spell to Find Lost Toys" and "Merlin's Spell to Make Broken Toys Happy" ~ Mike Jubb for "Some Day, My Prince", "Where Can It Be?" and "The Which Hoo Cudn't Spel" ~ Jean Kenward for "The King and Queen of China" and "The Path" ~ Patricia Leighton for "Dream Catcher", "Dreams and Shadows", "Magpie Magic" and "Who Believes in Fairies?" ~ The Literary Trustees of Walter de la Mare and the Society of Authors as their representative for "Eeka Neeka" by Walter de la Mare ~ Wes Magee for "Do You Want to Be a Wizard?" ~ Tony Mitton for "Cherry Croak", "Magic Carpet", "Merlin's Mynah", "Song of the Wizard's Imp" and "Tiny Elephants" ~ Lilian Moore for "Listen" ~ The National Exhibition of Children's Art, Poetry Section for "The Preston Witch" by Sara Jones and "Maybe Outside" by Cathy Vincent ~ Judith Nicholls for "Dragonbirth" ~ Peters, Fraser & Dunlop Group Ltd for "The Woman of Water" by Adrian Mitchell, from *Nothingmas Day,* pub. Allison & Busby ~ Tim Pointon for "The Vanishing Poem" ~ David Poulter for "Mummy?" ~ Laura Ranger for "Disappear", "Two Word Poem" and "Weed Soup" by permission of Godwit Publishing, New Zealand ~ The James Reeves Estate for "Little Fan" and "The Three Singing Birds" by James Reeves ~ John Rice for "Spell for Disappearing" ~ Daphne Schiller for "Broomstick Obedience Class" and "Wizard" ~ Charles Thomson for "Building a Dragon" ~ Jonathan Wakeham for "What My Granny Did" ~ Dave Ward for "Hallowe'en" from *Let's Celebrate*, pub. OUP ~ Celia Warren for "Lion" and "The Woolly Witch" ~ David Whitehead for "Hallowe'en Disco" and "Witchy Kittens" ~ Manley Young for "Anancy the Spiderman".